GLADIATORS

WARRIORS AROUND THE WORLD
GLADIATORS
SUSAN NICHOLS
Britannica
Educational Publishing

Published in 2017 by Britannica Educational Publishing (a trademark of Encyclopædia Britannica, Inc.) in association with The Rosen Publishing Group, Inc.
29 East 21st Street, New York, NY 10010

Distributed exclusively by Rosen Publishing.
To see additional Britannica Educational Publishing titles, go to rosenpublishing.com.

First Edition

Britannica Educational Publishing
J.E. Luebering: Executive Director, Core Editorial
Anthony L. Green: Editor, Compton's by Britannica

Rosen Publishing
Carolyn DeCarlo: Editor
Nelson Sá: Creative Director
Matt Cauli: Designer
Cindy Reiman: Photography Manager
Nicole Reinholdt: Photo Researcher

Library of Congress Cataloguing-in-Publication Data

Names: Nichols, Susan, 1975– author.
Title: Gladiators / Susan Nichols.
Description: First edition. | New York, NY : Britannica Educational Publishing in Association with Rosen Educational Services, 2017. | Series: Warriors around the world | Includes bibliographical references and index.
Identifiers: LCCN 2016020437 | ISBN 9781508103776 (library bound) | ISBN 9781508104339 (pbk.) | ISBN 9781508102991 (6-pack)
Subjects: LCSH: Gladiators—Juvenile literature.
Classification: LCC GV35 .N54 2016 | DDC 796.80937—dc23
LC record available at https://lccn.loc.gov/2016020437

Manufactured in China

Photo credits: Cover, p. 3 Luis Louro/Shutterstock.com; p. 7 Photos.com/Thinkstock; pp. 8-9 © Giakita/Alamy Stock Photo; pp. 10-11 Private Collection/© Look and Learn/Illustrated Papers Collection/Bridgeman Images; p. 13 Culture Club/Hulton Archive/Getty Images; p. 14 Stefano Bianchetti/Corbis Historical/Getty Images; p. 16 (inset) © 1960 Universal Pictures Company, Inc.; p. 18 Courtesy of the New York Public Library; p. 19 © Brenda Kean/age fotostock; p. 21 © Classic Image/Alamy Stock Photo; p. 22 (inset) Artephot/Pubbli Aer Foto; p. 23 Mondadori Portfolio/Hulton Fine Art Collection/Getty Images; p. 25 © Walker Art Library/Alamy Stock Photo; p. 26 DEA/G. Dagli Orti/De Agostini/Getty Images; p. 27 (inset) Heritage Images/Hulton Fine Art Collection/Getty Images; p. 29 Pictorial Press Ltd/Alamy Stock Photo; p. 31 Universal Images Group/Getty Images; p. 33 Three Lions/Hulton Archive/Getty Images; p. 35 © Peter Horree/Alamy Stock Photo; p. 38 Kachelhoffer Clement/Corbis Historical/Getty Images; p. 39 Museo Capitolino, Rome, Italy/Getty Images; pp. 40-41 (inset) © liszt collection/Alamy Stock Photo; interior pages border images © iStockphoto.com/slavazyryanov (fighting gladiators), © iStockphoto.com/gianlucabartoli (arches), ©iStockphoto.com/Ol`ga Myrontseva (shielded gladiator); pp. 16, 17, 22, 27, 32, 40, 41 (background) © iStockphoto.com.

Contents

INTRODUCTION

In the United States, Super Bowl Sunday is almost a national holiday. Many Americans celebrate this annual competition to see which professional gridiron football team is truly the best. Fans enjoy the thrill of celebrating with the winners or groaning with disappointment when their favored team doesn't succeed. Viewers feel very invested in the game; the same can be said of the World Series, the World Cup, and other sports competitions – it is truly enjoyable to watch matches between excellent competitors.

While sports fans today feel very connected to the game they are watching, this is nothing compared to the way in which Romans participated in the sporting event of their day: the gladiator games.

These enormous competitions took place in Rome between 264 BCE and 404 CE. In the great arena known as the Colosseum, men and women who had been training for years battled each other—but not for trophies or rings.

The prize for defeating their opponents was simple, but precious: they would live.

Sometimes, winners—especially if they were favorites of the fans or of the emperor—would be given a palm branch to symbolize victory, or even prize money. The greatest prize a gladiator could receive was a *rudis*, a wooden sword that symbolized liberty: the gladiator who was handed the rudis knew that he was now a free man.

But what of the loser? Their fate was often decided by the fans.

These thousands of Romans who crowded the Colosseum to watch the games actually played an important role in their

A Roman mosaic depicts gladiators in the midst of battle.

outcomes. The gladiator who lost the competition looked to them for his or her life to be spared. The crowd could "vote" in one of two ways.

The crowd might decide to spare the life of the gladiator, especially if he or she had put up a good fight or displayed heroism or bravery in some bold way. There are several ways a spectator could express his or her interest in sparing the loser. One was with the wave of a handkerchief; another, a popular hand gesture. The gesture used in this case was a *pollice compresso*, or "compressed thumb," in which the thumb is tucked or hidden inside the fist. This meant that the gladiator should live to compete another day.

Alternatively, *pollice verso*, which means "turned thumb" in Latin, was a gesture in which a person held up his hand with the thumb jutting out. Some historians have mistakenly said that the thumb was turned up, which

A* rudis *represented freedom to any gladiator awarded with the prize. As depicted here, the gladiator's name was inscribed in Latin on the blade.

led to the *thumbs up* gesture that means "good job" today, but this is not true; there is no documentation that supports the idea that the thumb was turned *up*, only *out*. Perhaps the thumb sticking out, in any direction, represented a stabbing motion, because the gladiator who received this gesture was usually put to death on the arena floor.

Crowds cheered as they watched the losing gladiator die. From

This engraving reproduces the famous painting Pollice Verso *by Jean-Léon Gérôme, in which a gladiator looks to the crowd for the fate of his opponent.*

evidence of this gleeful reaction, many historians agree that the era of the gladiator games in Rome was one of the bloodiest, most troubling in human history. This book will describe the lives of the gladiators and what they endured to compete in these games, in which winning meant everything.

Chapter 1
Who Were the Gladiators?

The gladiator games were costly, and not just in terms of human lives. They were grand affairs—massive festivals that were intended to entertain the citizens of Rome and the nearby towns. They could only have been put on by an empire that was very wealthy—and the Roman Empire was certainly one of the wealthiest in history.

Entertaining an Empire

The Romans began building their empire more than two thousand years ago, and at its greatest point, it included all of Europe—even Great Britain—and stretched across North Africa and into parts of Asia. The Romans conquered all of these lands because they had a powerful and efficient army. Rome produced the finest, deadliest weapons, and its massive army was big enough to protect the borders, stop rebellions, and maintain order among the many territories that became part of this vast empire.

All territories annexed to the empire were heavily controlled by Rome and paid taxes, in either gold or other resources. Egypt, for example, had abundant amounts of grain, which it paid regularly to the empire.

That money flowed into the capital city. Rome, located in modern-day Italy, had a population of approximately one million people

This map illustrates the Roman Empire at its peak, when it reached from the Iberian Peninsula in the west to most of the Middle East.

who demanded regular entertainment. The city leaders organized many events for the populace, including the gladiator games. The first known gladiatorial combat took place in 264 BCE in which three pairs of gladiators fought each other. Julius Caesar once hosted a competition in which 320 pairs of gladiators battled one another. The games became so popular, in fact, that most large cities across the empire eventually built their own arenas to host their own gladiator competitions.

Prisoners for Sport

Gladiators took their name from one of the weapons they commonly

This engraving by Heinrich Leutemann depicts one gladiator being defeated by his opponent. Both men are shown with the gladius, *a short sword commonly used in combat.*

used. The *gladius* was a short sword that could be used with deadly accuracy to kill one's opponent.

But who were these warriors? Who would compete in a game that could result in his or her own death?

Nobody competed willingly, of course. The gladiators were mostly prisoners of war. The massive Roman army often confronted nations who wanted to remain free from Roman rule; these populations were usually defeated easily. When the mighty Roman army conquered a new territory or suppressed a rebellion in an existing territory, the soldiers who had been defeated were either executed on the spot or captured as prisoners of war. Rather than languishing in cells, these captured soldiers were trained as gladiators—facing death either way.

Other gladiators were slaves who had been purchased or captured from across the Roman territories as well. Slavery in ancient Rome was a terrible system, and slaves were often treated cruelly. Slave status was not based on race; rather, slaves were usually non-Roman foreigners who were purchased to work in Roman households, build structures and aqueducts, or work as carpenters, masons, and farmers. Some educated slaves served as tutors and teachers to Roman children.

Still other gladiators were condemned criminals who were sent to train in gladiator schools as part of their sentence. These men would otherwise have been sentenced to death for their crimes; instead, the Roman government used them for entertainment purposes.

Most people assume gladiators were all men, but there were some

SPARTACUS

One of the Romans' biggest fears was slave rebellion, since slaves sometimes outnumbered free citizens three to one. In 73 BCE, one slave made that fear a reality.

Spartacus was a brave and bold man from Thrace, who had once served in the Roman army. He deserted the army—and eventually got caught. Desertion was a serious crime with serious consequences, and Spartacus was demoted to the status of a slave. Because he was strong, he was forced to become a gladiator and sent to the gladiator training center in Capua.

American actor Kirk Douglas starred in the 1960 film Spartacus, *based on the life of the slave who led an uprising against the Romans.*

Spartacus managed to escape from Capua and organize a formidable slave uprising. Eventually, Spartacus amassed a militia of runaway slaves, setting up headquarters near Mount Vesuvius. Because many of them were excellent fighters, they were able to fend off the Roman army for two years. In one cunning move, they hid in the cracks of the volcano and led a surprise attack on an approaching Roman battalion. Each time they won a battle, they took the defeated soldiers' weapons, handing them out to other slaves to encourage them to join their rebellion.

Spartacus's rebellion was finally defeated by the Roman commander Marcus Licinius Crassus, and Spartacus and 6,000 of his men were killed.

female warriors as well. Though it is unclear when women began to fight in the arena, it seems that many Romans did not like the idea. They thought that having women battle was an insult to the games, which were meant to celebrate masculine strength and prowess. However, according to historian Fik Meijer, in his book *Gladiators: History's Most Deadly Sport*, some emperors such as the emperor Nero must have encouraged the idea of female gladiators, "since women regularly fought in his shows."

It is important to remember that animals were also used in these bloody matches. Sometimes

This 1887 painting by Edwin Blashfield portrays female gladiators in combat.

a gladiator would compete against a lion, a bear, or other fearsome animals that were shipped to the Colosseum from across the empire. Animals were used in this way to showcase Roman strength, as a symbol of how vast the empire really was.

CHAPTER 2
LEARNING TO BE A WARRIOR

Young men (and some women)—after being captured, enslaved, or imprisoned—were forced into gladiator academies or schools. These academies were established in Rome in the first years after gladiator competitions became popular, and soon, there were several across the empire.

Here, they trained to perform in top physical condition and learned to handle weapons. Being sent to an academy probably felt

These are the ruins of Palestra, a gladiator training area in Pompeii, which was destroyed by the eruption of Mount Vesuvius in 79 CE.

like a death sentence to these youths, because the training they endured was so brutal it could kill them before they ever stepped into the arena.

Gladiator Academies

Upon entering the academy, the trainees were told that their personal lives and well-being did not matter anymore. Instead, obeying, working hard, and maintaining the academy's honorable reputation should be first priority. According to Meijer, the gladiator "swore a solemn oath (*sacramentum*) officially confirming his downgrading, promising to endure the worst kinds of humiliation and to suffer death by fire, in chains, or by the sword without protest."

Every school had a manager who supervised the academy. When a festival was planned and gladiators were required, people would contact the manager, who would decide which gladiators would be sent to fight. The academy would earn a profit from this business—another kind of slave trade in the Roman Empire.

Gladiators were taught by a magister, a man who helped them learn techniques for fighting, strategies for beating an opponent, and the ways to handle specific weapons. Magisters were usually brutal men who tried to extinguish any spark of rebellion in the gladiators; they forced them to train all day long, and sometimes at night.

Life in the Barracks

The gladiators slept in tiny barracks, and they were usually locked in so

An illustration of two gladiators at practice, while their trainer, or magister, stands behind them giving instructions.

they wouldn't escape. The academy had a small eating area, where the gladiators would take their meals, and a hospital to treat injuries during training. The weapons they used during the day for training were also locked up so that the gladiators couldn't get them to either escape or attack their trainers.

Meijer believes there may have been about one hundred academies

The Colosseum

The Colosseum is one of ancient Rome's most recognizable ruins. The large amphitheater was constructed between 70 and 72 CE. In 80 CE, it was opened to the public with one hundred days of games as a celebration. The amphitheater could seat fifty thousand spectators, and it stood three stories high. For four hundred years, the Colosseum was used for many public events, after which it fell into ruin and was used as a quarry, where stone for other construction projects would be mined. However, it eventually was recognized as an important Roman landmark and has since been preserved for historical purposes. Currently, it is one of Rome's most popular tourist sites.

The ruins of the Roman Colosseum, as seen today.

The connecting tunnel between the Colosseum and the Ludus Magnus, known as a cryptoporticus, is shown here.

across the empire; there were at least four in Rome itself. One of the largest academies was the Ludus Magnus. It was so large that it had its own seating around the practice arena, where approximately three thousand spectators could watch gladiators during their daily practices and training. The Ludus Magnus was located next to the Colosseum in Rome; in fact, gladiators could actually reach the Colosseum through a passageway that connected the Ludus Magnus to the arena where they would perform and fight.

Chapter 3
Types of Gladiators

According to Meijer, the earliest gladiators were known as Samnites and Galli warriors, probably because they were people who had been captured from the Roman provinces of Samnium (in modern-day Italy) and Gaul (in modern-day France). As the games became more and more popular, gladiators were differentiated by their weapons and fighting methods.

A Diverse Team

One kind of gladiator was the Retiarius, who fought with little protection. He was recognizable to the crowds because he carried only a trident and a net, with which he ensnared and brought down his opponents. He was often paired in exciting matches against a gladiator known as the Secutor, who was much more heavily armored. The Secutor wore a special helmet with small eyeholes to guard against the three sharp blades of the Retiarius' trident. According to Roger Dunkle, author of *Gladiators: Violence and Spectacle in Ancient Rome*, the battle between an armored Secutor and an unarmored but quick-footed Retiarius was very popular among the Roman spectators.

The Equites were gladiators who fought each other on horseback, carrying lances as well as swords. Dunkle writes, "It is clear that the Equites were real horsemen." He notes that many gladiatorial games opened with the Equites, who entered the arena from opposite ends,

An engraving that depicts two gladiators in battle. The man on the right, a Retiarius, carries a large trident and a net to ensnare his opponent.

riding white horses and carrying lances and small bronze shields. If an Equite were thrown off his horse, he could still fight on the ground, using either his lance or a small sword. Similarly, the Essedarii were gladiators who battled each other while riding on an *essedum*, a two-wheeled chariot. Like the Equites, they could start the battle on their chariots but finish it on foot.

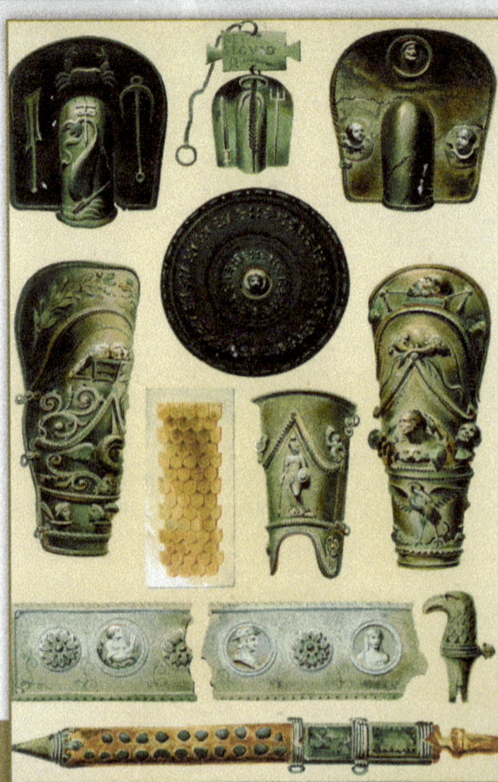

These reproductions of gladiators' weapons include leg armor, swords, and a circular shield known as a parmula.

The Thracians and Murmillones were two very popular types of gladiators. The Thracians carried a small shield called a *parmula*, which was round or square, and a sword with a curved blade called a *sica*. The Murmillones looked more like soldiers, carrying a *scutum*, a large shield in the shape of a rectangle, and the short gladius sword. Often pitted against one another, both the Thracians and Murmillones wore helmets that covered their faces for maximum protection. They also wore heavy armor plates on their arms, legs, and thighs to protect their limbs. In contrast,

CHARIOT RACES

One of the most exciting aspects of gladiator games to the Roman spectators were chariot races, which took place in the Colosseum or in the nearby Circus Maximus, a larger arena that could hold more spectators. The races featured chariots led by one driver and pulled by teams of two or four horses. In his book, *Empire of Ancient Rome*, Michael Burgan writes, "The drivers competed for one of four teams, distinguished by the color of their clothing: red, blue, green or white." Like gladiators, the drivers were slaves, who were often injured or killed when chariots collided.

Another painting by Jean-Léon Gérôme, The Circus Maximus, *portrays a chariot race in the famous racing stadium in Rome.*

their chests were left bare, adding to the tension and excitement for the audience, as the unarmored chest emphasized their true vulnerability. A gladiator fighting in this style would have to be very muscular and strong in order to be able to wear such heavy armor and still move around the arena.

The Provocator was another gladiator who looked much like the Thracian and the Murmillo, but he wore an armored breastplate. According to Dunkle, "No other type of gladiator wore protective armor on the chest."

There were many other types of gladiators, some of whom were used in the arena between serious matches to provide lighter entertainment. For example, older gladiators were used as Paegnarii, who were more like actors. According to Meijer, they fought each other using whips and hooked sticks, rather than heavy swords or lances.

Gladiators as Heroes

A point of interest in the history of the games is that despite the fact that gladiators' lives were not valued by the Romans, some became real heroes to the populace. In fact, some gladiators achieved genuine fame due to their many victories in the arena.

One of these heroes was Flavius Sigerus, who won so many battles that he continued fighting into his sixties. Flavius was awarded his freedom upon retiring from the arena; he was so proud of this fact that he had it engraved on his tombstone. Other famous gladiators included Auctus, a warrior who is recorded as having

Russell Crowe starred in the action-packed 2000 film Gladiator, *the fictional portrayal of a heroic general-turned-gladiator named Maximus.*

50 wins, and Asteropaeus, a gladiator who amassed an incredible 107 victories. However, Meijer reminds us that "the vast majority of gladiators" died before they were thirty years old.

Chapter 4
The Real Lives of the Gladiators

Many Romans romanticized the gladiator as a man of dignity who fought with honor. They packed the Colosseum's seating, cheering for their favorite fighters. Many also attended daily practice sessions at the Ludus Magnus, watching the grueling practices. Children pretended to be gladiators and fought with wooden swords, and they played with small clay dolls shaped like their favorite warriors. The gladiator culture was deeply entrenched in Roman society.

A Difficult Life

Despite this romanticization, gladiators were some of the lowest ranking people in Roman society; after all, most of them were condemned criminals, slaves, or prisoners of war. While a few achieved fame, most died at a very young age–and died cruel deaths, at that.

Gladiators' daily lives were stressful and tragic. It is difficult to imagine a gladiator, practicing every day at his academy, training with others who might one day kill him in the arena. He slept in barracks with other fighters, against whom he might well be paired to fight to the death in the near future.

Gladiators fought two or three times a year. In each fight, there was a chance they could win and live and a chance they would be killed. A

Roman children played with toys, too. Here is a clay puppet, fashioned in the shape of a Roman soldier.

gladiator could die in several ways: he could be defeated by his opponent and killed on the arena floor; he could die of his wounds after the match ended; he could lose a match and be condemned to death by

Roman Virtues

Despite the stressors on their own lives, gladiators were glorified by a society that perhaps didn't want to know the truth. Gladiators were revered as men who represented certain Roman virtues:

Fortitudo, the Latin term for courage, was one of the most highly valued Roman virtues. Gladiators possessed this in abundance. They also possessed *disciplina*, the Latin term for discipline, because of their rigorous training. They also displayed disciplina by obeying the regulations of gladiator matches, even when it came to their own deaths; a gladiator who had been sentenced to death was expected to—and usually did—kneel down and accept their fate without complaint.

Gladiators also displayed what the Romans called *contemptus mortis*, which Meijer translates as "fearlessness in the face of death." This, of course, must be viewed with skepticism by historians today; most gladiators were terrified of dying, but because they were essentially slaves, they had no other choice but to fight.

the audience; he could die during a physically taxing training session; or he could die while trying to escape.

The stress of their lives was so great that suicide was not uncommon among gladiators. In one recorded match, twenty gladiators committed mass suicide rather than battle one another.

A group of gladiators salute the Roman emperor before the beginning of the games, a reminder that they were slaves and subject to his authority.

The Brotherhood of the Collegia

Some gladiators bonded over their dismal fate. They formed a kind of brotherhood, in which they comforted one another. These eventually became "formal unions," or *collegia*, in which the gladiators promised to take care of one another.

For example, when a gladiator was killed in the arena, the members of the collegia made sure that he was given a proper funeral. This was one of the most important benefits of a collegia membership. In fact, they buried him with specific honors, marking his gravestone with his achievements.

Some evidence shows that gladiators' bodies may have been used to feed the wild animals used in the games. Otherwise, as many gladiators were slaves or criminals, their bodies were simply tossed into the woods or into a river. As Meijer explains, "The most humiliating fate that could befall a gladiator after his death was to be given no funeral at all. His body would not be covered with earth, which meant, so the Romans believed, that his soul could never find peace." A proper burial was significant to the gladiators, who had so little hope in their short lives.

If a fallen gladiator had a wife and children, the collegia provided his family with money to help alleviate their financial stress. This was also a comfort to the gladiators, who worried that their families would be condemned to poverty after their deaths.

The members of a collegia worshipped the same god or goddess, to whom they prayed to watch over

The gravestone of this gladiator indicates that he was a Retiarius, trained to fight with a net.

and protect them. They also elected representatives and leaders who would take care of the business matters of the gladiators.

Magisters and academy managers typically approved of the existence of the collegia, because it provided emotional comfort for the gladiators; it was in the interest of the magisters and managers to have fighters who would be steady and stable. In fact, they took great pains to make sure that gladiators were rarely left alone before matches, for fear that they would find a way to end their own lives.

Chapter 5

The End of the Gladiator Era

The Colosseum, where Romans flocked to see the gladiator games, held regular festivals and competitions. Festivals lasted from sunrise to sunset, and they usually began with chariot shows. The gladiators would then enter and salute the emperor, who presided over the festival from a raised seat. They would honor the emperor by saying, *Ave, imperator, morituri te salutant*! This is translated as "Hail, Emperor, those who are about to die salute you!"

The Festival Program

The Colosseum's morning schedule continued with dramas, comic shows and fights; sometimes, female gladiators competed in these. Next came the animal hunts, featuring wild animals such as bears, tigers, and even hippopotami.

At midday, executions would be held. The Roman Empire persecuted groups who were deemed a threat to their way of life, such as Christians. Alongside criminals, these groups found themselves subject to public execution.

Later in the afternoon, the gladiator games were held. This was the most exciting part of the festival, drawing the largest crowds. At the end of a typical festival day, those who worked in the Colosseum

A 1584 illustration of Tertullian by Andre Thevet, showing the Christian author engaged in reading and writing. Tertullian is referred to as the "Founder of Western Theology" because of the many Christian ideas he introduced.

had a gruesome task to complete. Before the next morning, the arena of the amphitheater had to be cleaned of all the blood that had been spilled throughout the day.

A Swelling Tide of Dissent

A marble bust of Marcus Tullius Cicero, a Roman philosopher, writer, and politician who lived from 106-43 BCE.

Over time, critical opinion over the gruesome gladiator games and the culture surrounding the festivals swelled. There had always been some critics of the games, including educated elite men like Cicero, who found the cruel and bloody nature of the games uncivilized. His objections were not based in human rights, but had more to do with an expectation that intelligent people should not be amused by such disgusting shows. Such blood sport was something that only "common" or lower-class people would find amusing, in Cicero's opinion.

Telemachus Protests the Gladiator Games

According to some historians, Emperor Honorius finally banned gladiator games in 404 CE because of the actions of Telemachus, a Christian monk. During an event in the

Colosseum, Telemachus bravely attempted to stop the battle. He jumped down from his seat and ran onto the arena floor. Despite the swords and weapons swinging around him, he tried to separate the two gladiators.

The crowd, which had been waiting all day for the gladiator games, became enraged at this interruption. A mob jumped onto the arena floor and attacked Telemachus, killing him before anyone could help him.

Honorius, who was present and saw the murder of Telemachus, put an end to gladiator competitions.

Telelmachus was later declared a saint in the Christian church.

This 1701 depiction of the stoning of Saint Telemachus during a Roman gladiatorial battle was created by Jan Luyken.

Christians, on the other hand, challenged the gruesome treatment of other human beings in the gladiator games. Tertullian, one of the earliest Christian theologians, wrote an important work, *De Spectaculis*, in approximately 200 CE. In this treatise, he argued that Christians should never attend the gladiator games and festivals because it was morally wrong to find pleasure in the suffering of another person.

Despite their opponents' best efforts, Christianity spread slowly throughout the Roman Empire. In 313 CE, Emperor Constantine issued the Edict of Milan, which began the conversion of the Roman Empire to Christianity. Emperor Honorius banned gladiator academies in 399 CE, and by 404 CE, he had put an end to the games in full.

GLOSSARY

arena The central area in the Colosseum where gladiator matches and other events took place.

Colosseum A large, open-air building, which still stands today; the location of most major festivals and gladiator competitions in Rome.

collegia Unions formed by gladiators.

contemptus mortis The Roman virtue of "fearlessness in the face of death."

cupido victoraie The Roman virtue of "will to win."

disciplina The Roman virtue of discipline.

edict A law, usually passed by an authority such as an emperor.

empire A system of government in which territories are subjected to the control of another, more powerful territory.

essedum A two-wheeled chariot, often used in gladiatorial matches by the Essedarii.

fortitudo The Roman virtue of courage.

gladiator A warrior who fought in competitions usually for the entertainment of the populace.

gladius A short sword used in battles, from which the term gladiator is derived.

parmula A small shield carried by Thracian gladiators.

pollice compresso The "hidden thumb" gesture used by crowds to signal that a gladiator's life should be spared.

pollice verso The "turned thumb" gesture used by crowds to signal that a gladiator should be executed.

Retiarius A type of gladiator mostly unprotected by armor and who carried only a net and a trident during his fight.

rudis A wooden stick given rarely as a prize to a winning gladiator; it symbolized that he'd won his freedom.

scutum A shield in the shape of a rectangle carried by Murmillone gladiators.

sica A sword with a curved blade carried by Thracian gladiators.

slaves Individuals who are owned by another person and forced to work or serve against their will.

FOR FURTHER READING

Burgan, Michael. *Empire of Ancient Rome*. New York, NY: Chelsea House, 2009.

Dunkle, Roger. *Gladiators: Violence and Spectacle in Ancient Rome*. New York, NY: Routledge, 2013.

Ganeri, Anita. *How to Live Like a Roman Gladiator*. Minneapolis, MN: Hungry Tomato, 2015.

Hayes, Oliver. *The Roman Gladiator Referee's Handbook*. Epsom, UK: Bretwalda Books, 2013.

Hoblin, Paul. *Gladiators: Great Warriors*. Edina, MN: Core Library, 2013.

Hyde, Natalie. *Gladiators*. New York, NY: Crabtree Publishing, 2016.

James, Simon. *Ancient Rome: DK Eyewitness Books*. New York, NY: DK Publishing, 2015.

Lee, Adrienne. *Gladiators: Legendary Warriors*. North Mankato, MN: Capstone Press, 2015.

Macdonald, Fiona. *The Roman Colosseum: Spectacular Visual Guides*. Brighton, UK: Scribo Books, 2015.

Malam, John. *You Wouldn't Want to Be a Roman Gladiator!: Gory Things You'd Rather Not Know*. London, UK: Franklin Watts, 2012.

Mattern, Joanne. *Gladiators: Warriors Graphic Illustrated*. Vero Beach, FL: Rourke Publishing, 2011.

Matthews, Rupert. *100 Facts: Gladiators*. Thaxted, UK: Miles Kelly Publishers, 2015.

Matthews, Rupert. *Gladiators: History's Fearless Fighters.* New York, NY: Gareth Stevens Publishing, 2015.

Matyszak, Philip. *Gladiator: The Roman Fighter's [Unofficial] Manual.* London, UK: Thames & Hudson, 2011.

Meijer, Fik. *Gladiators: History's Most Deadly Sport.* New York, NY: St Martin's Press, 2004.

Pierce, Nick. *Gladiator: Death and Glory in Ancient Rome.* Brighton, UK: Scribo Books, 2016.

West, David. *Lots of Things You Want to Know About Gladiators... and Some You Don't!* Mankato, MN: Smart Apple Media, 2016

Websites

Because of the changing nature of internet links, Rosen Publishing has developed an online list of websites related to the subject of this book. This site is updated regularly. Please use this link to access this list:

http://www.rosenlinks.com/WAW/gladi

Index